For five dogs past and present—
Johnny Bull
Gretchen
Casey
Ladi
Ophelia

Clarion Books
a Houghton Mifflin Company imprint
215 Park Avenue South, New York, NY 10003
Text and illustrations copyright © 1993 by Eileen Christelow

Library of Congress Cataloging-in-Publication Data
Christelow, Eileen.
The five-dog night / by Eileen Christelow.
p.   cm.
Summary: Cantankerous Ezra keeps rebuffing his nosy neighbor Old
Betty when she tries to give him advice on how to survive the cold
winter nights, until she finally discovers that his five dogs are
his private source for warmth.
ISBN 0-395-62399-5   PA ISBN 0-395-92862-1
[1. Winter—Fiction.   2. Neighborliness—Fiction.   3. Dogs—
Fiction.]   I. Title.   II. Title: 5-dog night.
PZ7.C4523Fi   1993
[E]—dc20   92-36958
CIP
AC
WOZ 10 9 8 7 6 5 4

The Five-Dog Night

written and illustrated by
EILEEN CHRISTELOW

CLARION BOOKS · NEW YORK

Ezra lived alone in a small house, high on a windy hilltop. Well, not exactly alone...he had five dogs for company.

And halfway down the hill lived old Betty. She visited Ezra almost every day, rain or shine. Ezra loved his dogs, but he figured he could pretty much take or leave old Betty.

When Ezra saw her climbing up the hill to his house, he grumbled to his dogs, "Here comes that old busybody, Betty."

As soon as he said that, all five dogs were up and running down the hill. They barked. They wagged their tails. They licked Betty's face.

She gave them each a cookie.

"Humph!" grumbled Ezra. "You spoil those dogs. They're supposed to chase you away."

"Posh!" said Betty. "I brought you some cookies, too. I'll make us a pot of tea."

"Don't bother yourself," said Ezra. But Betty made tea.

"Fall is here," she said. "The leaves are turning. It's going to be chilly tonight. You'll need an extra blanket."

"I don't need blankets," said Ezra.

"Everyone needs blankets," said Betty.

"Not me," said Ezra, his mouth full of cookies.

"Stubborn as a mule," said Betty as she headed home.

"Nosy as a mouse sniffing for cheese," Ezra muttered as he fed the dogs.

That night, a chill breeze blew in from the north. Down in her house, Betty put an extra blanket on her bed.

But, up in his house, Ezra did not need an extra blanket.

The next morning, Betty climbed the hill to visit Ezra.

"Chilly last night," said Betty.

"Wasn't too bad," said Ezra. "It was only a one-dog night."

"What are you talking about?" said Betty.

Ezra just winked at the dogs.

"Crazy as a loon!" said Betty.

"Nosy old biddy," Ezra muttered.

During the next weeks all the leaves turned red and gold. Then one day a wind came up and it rained, knocking the last of the leaves from the trees.

Betty told Ezra, "Winter is coming. I hear it's going to clear up tonight and get so cold there'll be ice on the puddles by morning. You'll surely need a blanket."

"Nope," said Ezra. "I won't."

That night was so chilly, Betty had to get up at two A.M. to find another blanket. She could just see Ezra's house in the moonlight.

"That stubborn old mule is probably up there shivering and quivering with the cold," she said to herself.

But, up in his house, Ezra was not shivering and quivering with the cold.

The next day, Ezra was carrying in wood for his stove when Betty came up the hill to visit.

"Cold last night," said Betty. "The last of my garden froze up, shriveled, and died."

"It wasn't so bad," said Ezra. "It was only a two-dog night."

"Humph!" said Betty. "Talking crazy again. But you better cover up tonight. They say a snowstorm is coming our way."

"I'm not worried," said Ezra.

That night, the first snow fell.
Down in her house, Betty took out her winter quilt.

But, up in his house, Ezra didn't need any winter quilts.

The next morning, Betty put on her boots and her heavy winter coat, and she climbed the hill to check on Ezra. He was warming himself by the wood stove.

"I brought you a blanket," said Betty.

"I don't use blankets," said Ezra. "I said it before. I'll say it again."

"It was freezing cold last night!" said Betty. "You'll catch pneumonia!"

"It wasn't so bad," said Ezra. "It was only a three-dog night."

"Gibberish!" said Betty. "That's all *that* is! But the weather is going to get worse. You'll need this blanket soon."

The next couple of weeks, it snowed again and then
again. In fact the snow got so deep, it reached halfway up
Ezra's windows.

Then one night an icy north wind blew the clouds from the
sky, uncovering the stars. The temperature dropped to zero.

But Ezra didn't use Betty's blanket.

The next morning, Betty chugged up the hill in her car to visit Ezra. She brought hot chocolate in a thermos.

"It's too cold to walk," she said. "It was freezing last night! Did you use the blanket?"

"Nope," said Ezra. "It was only a four-dog night."

"The colder it gets, the crazier you get!" said Betty.

"You mean the colder it gets, the nosier YOU get," mumbled Ezra.

The next days were so cold the trees cracked and the river froze solid.

Then one evening an Arctic wind howled around Ezra's house. The temperature dropped well below zero. Even Ezra's largest and furriest dog would not stay outside.

Betty piled all of her blankets and coats onto her bed. She stoked her wood stove with extra logs.

"Ezra will have to stoke his wood stove all night," she thought as she shivered under her blankets. "And he'll have to use that blanket, or he'll turn into a block of ice."

The next morning, Betty was so concerned about Ezra that she drove up to his house just as the sun was rising, before she had even eaten breakfast.

There was no smoke coming out of Ezra's chimney.

"No fire in the wood stove!" said Betty. "He's frozen to death!"

She opened Ezra's door and peeked inside—and there was Ezra, snoring happily without any blankets on at all. The dogs raised their heads and growled.

"Sh-h-h-h! It's only me!" whispered Betty.

The dogs jumped off the bed, barked, and wagged their tails. Ezra woke up.

"What's going on?" he asked.

"I was just checking to see if you're all right," said Betty.

"Well, DON'T!" roared Ezra. "You...you nosy old busybody!"

"If that's the way you feel, I won't—ever again!" shouted Betty. "You...you old grouch!"

She walked out of the house, slammed the door, and drove back down the hill.

"Well, I guess that old busybody won't nose around here again," Ezra told the dogs. "Good riddance!"

Not one tail wagged.

Weeks went by. The weather turned warmer. The snow melted. The dogs lay around in the front yard, watching the road. Betty didn't come up the hill.

"Awfully quiet around here," Ezra said to the dogs. "It's almost spring, and I'm feeling gloomy as a stormy sky. Can't figure it out."

Around the time the first daffodils were poking out of the ground, Ezra baked some cookies. Then he put on his cleanest shirt and walked down the hill. The dogs came with him.

Within earshot of Betty's house, they were greeted by the sound of barking.

Five dogs exploded out of Betty's gate and raced up the
road toward them. Betty came after them.

"Quiet!" she shouted. "Stop!"

"New dogs?" said Ezra.

"Got them in January," said Betty. "They are better company than some people I know."

"I can brew a pot of tea to go with these cookies I made," said Ezra. "Don't know of any dogs who can do that."

"Guess that's true," said Betty.

"It's a little warmer," said Ezra as he boiled water for tea.

"It certainly is," said Betty. "Last night was only a one-dog night."

"You'll catch your death of pneumonia!" said Ezra. "Last night was a two-dog night!"